I DON'T LIKE RAIN!

Sarah Dillard

Aladdin

NEW YORK LONDON TORONTO SYDNEY NEW DELHI

For Frankie Bigs

ALADDIN
An imprint of Simon & Schuster
Children's Publishing Division · 1230 Avenue of the
Americas, New York, New York 10020 · First Aladdin
hardcover edition March 2020 · Copyright © 2020
by Sarah Dillard · All rights reserved, including the right of
reproduction in whole or in part in any form. · ALADDIN and related logo
are registered trademarks of Simon & Schuster, Inc. · For information about
special discounts for bulk purchases, please contact Simon & Schuster Special Sales at
1-866-506-1949 or business@simonandschuster.com. · The Simon & Schuster Speakers
Bureau can bring authors to your live event. For more information or to book an event contact the
Simon & Schuster Speakers Bureau at 1-866-248-3049 or visit our website at www.simonspeakers.com.
Book designed by Laura Lyn DiSiena · The illustrations for this book were rendered digitally. · The text of this book
was hand-lettered. · Manufactured in China 1219 SCP · 2 4 6 8 10 9 7 5 3 1 · Library of Congress Control Number 2019936818 ·
ISBN 978-1-5344-0678-0 (hc) · ISBN 978-1-5344-0679-7 (eBook)

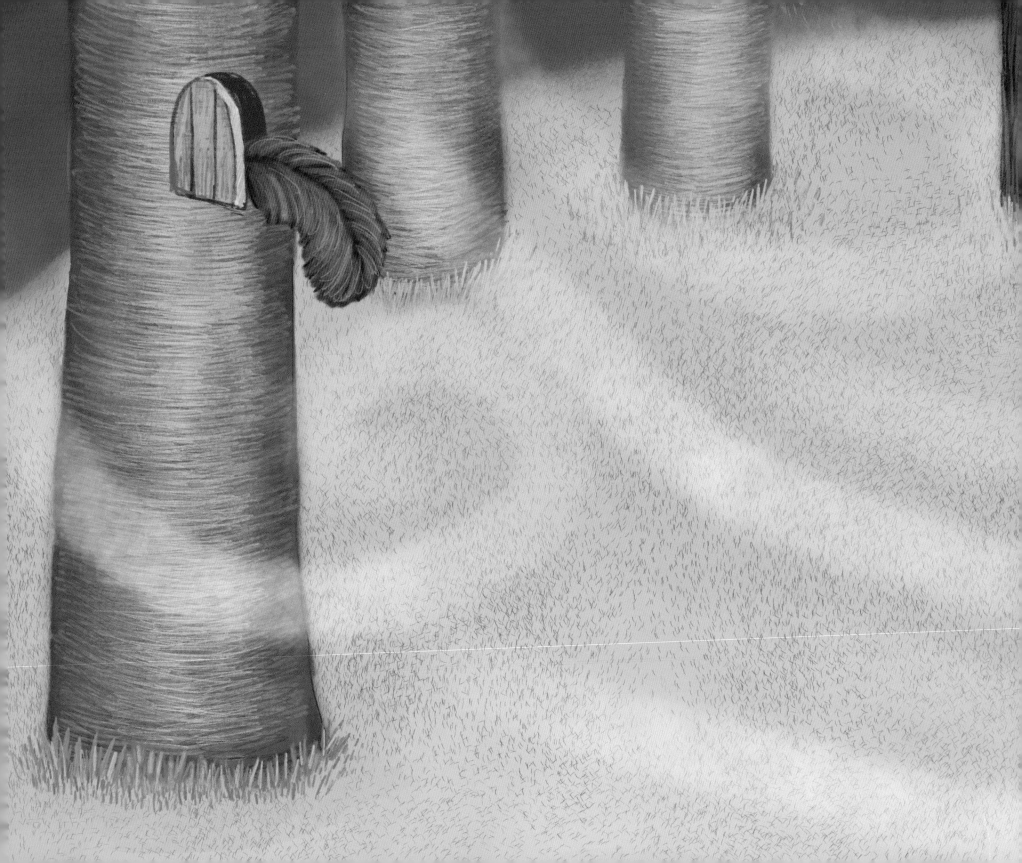

Drip.

Drip.

Drop.

Drip drip   drip drip   drip drip

drip drip   drip drip   drip drip

Drip,

drip,

drip,

drop.

Plop.

Flop.

Splish!

Splash!

Splish!

Splash!

Splash!

Splash, splash!

Splash, splash, splash!

Splash,
splash,
splash!

Splash,
splash!

Splash!

Splash!

Splash,
splash,
splash, splash,
splash,
splash!

Splash, splash, drip, drip.

Drip. Drip. Drip.